THE IMMORTAL

Other Books by the Author:

The Girl of the Alamo
    Story of Suzanna Dickinson

Juan Seguin
    A Hero of Texas

THE IMMORTAL

THIRTY-TWO MEN FROM GONZALES
ANSWERED THE PLEA FROM THE ALAMO

Rita Kerr

EAKIN PRESS ★ Austin, Texas

Library of Congress Cataloging-in-Publication Data

Kerr, Rita.
    The immortal thirty-two.

    Summary: Thirty-two men answer Colonel William Travis's plea for help
and cross enemy lines to help defend the Alamo in 1836.
    1. Texas — History — To 1846 — Juvenile fiction. [1. Texas — History — To
1846 — Fiction. 2. Alamo (San Antonio, Tex.) — Siege, 1836 — Fiction] I. Title.
II. Title: Immortal 32.
PZ7.K468458Im 1986   [Fic]   86-2071
ISBN 0-89015-538-0

This book is dedicated to the thirty-two brave men of Gonzales who rode to the aid of their fellow Texans besieged at the Alamo. Fully aware of their peril, these thirty-two heroes crossed the enemy lines and entered the Alamo on March 1, 1836. For six days they fought beside their comrades until overwhelmed and killed by Santa Anna's army. Their self-sacrifice and valor made them heroes of Texas. Their names, as shown below, appear on the monument in front of the Historical Museum of Gonzales, as well as the Alamo Monument in front of the State's Capitol, and the Alamo.

Albert Martin	James George
Isaac Baker	Thomas Jackson
John Cane	Johnny Kellogg
George Cottle	Andrew Kent
David Cummings	George C. Kimball
Squire Damon	John G. King
Jacob Darst	William P. King
John Davis	Jonathan Lindley
William Dearduff	Jesse McCoy
Charles Despallier	Thomas Miller
William Fishbaugh	Isaac Millsaps
John Flanders	George Neggan
Dolphin W. Floyd	William Summers
Galba Fuqua	George Tumlinson
John E. Garvin	Robert White
John E. Gaston	Claiborne Wright

PREFACE

The history of early Texas has many unnamed
heroes who fought and died that Texas might be
free. Among those were the people of Gonzales and
the thirty-two brave men who went to the Alamo in
response to Colonel William Travis's plea for help.
This is their story.

With Gratitude

The author wishes to express her gratitude to a
number of dedicated librarians for their assistance.
Special thanks to Maudine Harris, Peggy Lither-
bury, and the librarians at the DRT Alamo Library.
Sincere thanks goes to the citizens of Gonzales including Wayne Ellison, Barbara Hand, Ginny Kar-
los, Raguet Floyd, and Perry Bell.
The author expresses her appreciation to Ed
Eakin, publisher of Eakin Press, for his encourage-
ment and confidence in her ability; and to editor

Shirley Ratisseau for her creative guidance as consultant extraordinary.

Finally, the author gives special thanks to her husband for his gentle prodding and practical suggestions during the writing of *The Immortal Thirty-two*. Without these people and interested friends this book would not have been written.

ABOUT THE AUTHOR

Rita Kerr is a graduate of San Antonio College and Trinity University. She is a member of a number of organizations including: Texas Library Association, Texas Publishers Association, San Antonio Genealogical and Historical Society, and has worked with the San Antonio Sesquicentennial committee. Rita was a teacher in the San Antonio Independent School District for a number of years. Upon retirement she started a new career as a writer of historical books for children. Much of the author's time is now devoted to lecturing about early Texas. Dressed in pioneer clothing, she discusses her exhibit of artifacts and pictures. A sixth generation Texan, Rita endeavors to make history come alive for her audiences. Among the author's interests are church work, sewing and painting.

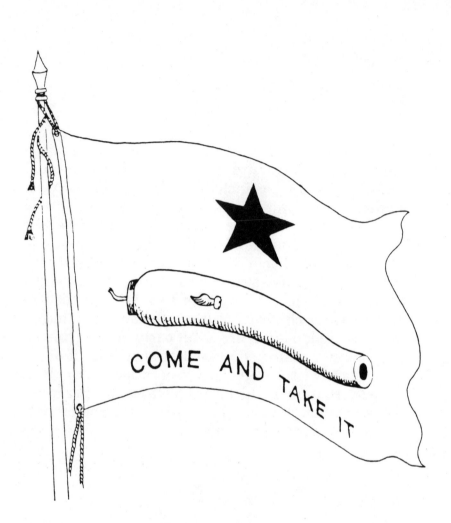

The Gonzales Flag

The Cannon

"John, we're counting on you as the lookout. You must keep your eyes open! Most of the men have taken their families to safety, and we've only eighteen fellows left in town. They'll be needed if there's trouble." Joseph Clement's solemn face emphasized the seriousness of the situation. "It's your job, boy, to warn us if you see anything unusual. Do you understand?"

The sixteen-year-old nodded. "Yes, sir, I understand. You can count on me."

The man's voice was grim as he went on. "I hope so. Our very lives and the future of this town depend on you. Now," he placed his hand on the boy's shoulder as he spoke. "Give me your gun and get up in the tree." Joseph Clements watched him shinny skillfully up the trunk of the huge oak and crawl to a large limb dangling overhead. "Here's your rifle, John, but don't use it unless you have to. I'll leave you now, but remember — give a yell if you see anything."

"I will, Mr. Clements." John watched the man until he disappeared behind the clump of trees near the town's square.

With his weapon balanced across his knees, John Gaston leaned back against the tree trunk. He had a panoramic view of the countryside from his perch high above the ground.

The teenager scratched his head and studied the scene. Everything looked normal. There was a hint of fall in the gentle breeze that rustled through the branches. The brightly colored gold and orange leaves signaled the end of another Texas summer. Wisps of smoke drifted up from the nearby cabins and vanished in the cloudless sky. With the final days of September, the year 1835 was passing quickly. John wondered what the future might hold for Gonzales.

The little town now boasted some thirty homes, with more in the outlying areas. Like other pioneer settlements, Gonzales had faced many struggles. Life in early Texas was not easy for those living in the colony founded by Green DeWitt in 1825. DeWitt was one of several leaders, or *empresarios,* to whom the Mexican government had granted permission to bring families from the States to settle in that area of Mexico called Texas.

It was common knowledge that DeWitt's American Colony was not the only one. Stephen Austin had brought 300 families and they had settled on the Brazos River. Still another settlement was near the Mexican village of Nacogdoches on the Texas–Louisiana border. Other colonies were the Power and Hewetson Colony and the Robertson Colony.

Empresario DeWitt had selected his location carefully. It was to be the most western settlement of immigrants from the United States in Texas. It was an ideal site with plenty of animal life, fertile soil, and beautiful trees. The Guadalupe River supplied clean, clear water for the original families who came with DeWitt. The settlers claimed their land and set about cutting trees for their cabins. The people worked hard, never thinking that their efforts might be doomed. But the first settlement of Gonzales met with a tragic fate.

John knew the story by heart. DeWitt had been out of town when the Indians swooped down on Gonzales. The settlers who were not killed in the surprise attack, ran for their lives. Most of their homes were burned. After the raid, the settlers abandoned the settlement for fear the Indians would return.

Dewitt would not give up. He was determined to rebuild. With the promise of rich land and a new life, he later brought more than one hundred families to Gonzales from Tennessee, Kentucky, North Carolina, and other states. John's folks, the George Davises, had been in the group. In return for land, the settlers promised to be loyal citizens of Mexico. They also agreed to uphold the laws of the Mexican Constitution of 1824, and to establish schools where their children could learn Spanish.

John's real father had died when he was small and his mother had remarried. John had heard his family talk about the journey to Texas. Although he was young, he could remember the awful wagon ride. It had been slow and bumpy. There were no roads. The trails were hard or impossible to follow. John's boyhood dreams were haunted by the nightmarish struggle to cross rivers swollen with rain and with the water swirling around the bed of the wagon. Once they rolled onto solid land, the paths were a sea of mud that clogged the wheels, stuck to shoes, and spattered clothes. John knew he would always hate sticky, gooey, mud! He never knew which was worse — rain or mud. As if those two things weren't hardship enough, many of the settlers became ill.

To add to their misery, the weather turned cold, and food was scarce. The days were difficult, but the nights were worse. The darkness brought frightening noises that made the children shiver with fear. John wasn't the only one with unhappy memories of that journey; many had buried loved ones along the way.

Day after day they had traveled. John had wondered if they would ever stop. Finally, after endless weeks of travel, they reached the rolling prairie along the Guadalupe River. Here was Gonzales, DeWitt's site for their new home.

The second group of colonists, like the first, battled the blazing sun to chop trees for their homes and clear the land. John's father planted the corn and wheat seed he had brought with them. He knew their future depended on those seeds. Without corn there would be no bread, no mush, no food for their animals. The dangers of snakes, coyotes, bears, and other creatures bothered John's mother. But the worst fear was of another Indian attack. Like the other women, John's mother was relieved when the Mexican government gave the town a small cannon — a six-pounder — in 1831. There were fewer Indian raids after that.

Life in Gonzales had been quiet until the new Mexican President took office. General Lopez de Santa Anna had made many changes. The Mexican leader raised taxes and passed laws the Texans did not like. These changes made them nervous. Often, the Texans talked of freedom and justice. John tried to understand their talk, but it wasn't easy.

With a yawn, John Gaston shifted his position on the limb. He wondered what was going to happen now. Four days ago, five Mexican soldiers and a Corporal De Leon suddenly appeared on the opposite side of the Guadalupe. The townsfolk were furious when the corporal demanded the return of their cannon. Andrew Ponton, the *alcalde* of the colony, had stationed guards to stall the Mexican soldiers down at the river so he could call a town meeting to discuss the situation.

John closed his eyes and pictured the people gathered around Ponton. He could see the men: Albert Martin, Almeron Dickinson, John's brother-in-law Johnny Kellogg, Jacob Darst, John Sowell, John's stepfather George Davis, Jesse McCoy, Andrew Kent, and the others. The women and children had stood around the edge of the group.

John always marveled at the varying sizes and shapes and ages of the men when they were together. Three of the tallest were Tennesseans who were as different as night from day. Almeron Dickinson was a cleanshaven muscular blacksmith in his mid-twenties, whereas Jacob Darst was a farmer whose graying beard partly concealed his aging weather-lined face. The third man from Tennessee, Thomas Miller, was a hatter. Miller's fine clothes and neat appearance looked strange beside the buckskins worn by the others.

John remembered how *Alcalde* Ponton had cleared his throat and said, "You know there are Mexican soldiers on the other side of our river. Corporal De Leon has orders from Colonel Ugartechea, the Mexican commander in San Antonio de Bexar, demanding the return of our cannon."

5

"That's our cannon! Why should we give it back?" John was proud of his father's words.

"I agree with you, Davis," the mayor shuffled his feet and twisted the end of his mustache nervously as he went on. "The way I see it, we haven't much choice but to give it back unless we want trouble. Of course, who's to say the Indians won't go on the warpath again? If they did, we'd need that cannon. That's for sure!"

Almeron Dickinson spoke up, "Why do they want our cannon anyway? They have better ones than ours in San Antonio right now. It seems to me that President Santa Anna is thinkin' of makin' himself a dictator! Next thing we know he'll be demandin' our guns. Then what will we do? Would we lay them down and say 'come and take em'? Why, then we'd be defenseless against the Indians and Santa Anna!"

Alcalde Ponton looked from face to face as he asked, "Anybody got any suggestions?"

One after another the men voiced their opinions. They finally decided the best way to keep the Mexican soldiers from getting their cannon was to hide it. Kellogg's suggestion to bury it brought a round of laughter. But, after much talking, they finally agreed that burying it wasn't such a bad idea after all.

John's father, George Davis, said no one would think of looking for a cannon in his peach orchard. The Darst children giggled at that.

A brief silence followed. Then Andrew Ponton spoke up. "Davis, that sounds like a good idea! We'll accept your offer. Your peach orchard will be a fine hiding place. Darst, you and Sowell go to George's orchard and help John Chisholm dig a big hole. Any other suggestions?"

Dickinson rubbed his chin thoughtfully and said, "We know the river's too high from the rains for that corporal to cross without a boat, and we've got the boats! Why don't some of us sneak over in our ferry and capture them? We could hold them in the compound at the fort until we see what's goin' to happen."

After much discussion, the men had taken Dickinson's suggestion and captured the Mexican soldiers without much trouble. Somehow, in the excitement, one of the Mexicans had escaped and headed back to San Antonio. Once the other prisoners were locked inside the fort, Ponton wrote a letter to the Mexican officials in hopes of changing their minds about the cannon. But the *alcalde* wasn't taking any chances. He sent Matthew Caldwell to alert the surrounding settlements to their problems. Dickinson and Sowell were instructed to pull the ferry boats up on the land to prevent anyone from crossing without warning. After that, most of the men, including Ponton, had taken their families to safety. It seemed certain Gonzales would soon hear from Colonel Ugartechea. John knew that was why he was up in the tree. He was to sound an alarm if he saw anything strange.

"I surely would like to stretch my legs," John muttered to himself as he studied the countryside. Suddenly, a flash of light caught his attention. The boy stared at the spot. He wondered if he had been dreaming. Yet, John was sure he had seen something. What could it have been? At the moment he decided he must have been mistaken, he saw the light again. This time he knew what it was: the light

7

was the sun's reflection on a bayonet carried by a Mexican soldier! As John watched, soldier after soldier rode into view until a large body of Mexican cavalrymen were assembled on the other side of the river. A brightly uniformed officer on a black horse led the troop.

John came to life. Scrambling down the tree, he hit the ground at a dead run. When he neared the town square, he yelled, "They're here! The whole Mexican army's come for our cannon!"

The town sprang to life. Men poured into the square from all directions to hear the boy's report.

"I saw them — I saw the Mexican soldiers at the river!" John shouted breathlessly as he came to an abrupt halt in front of the group.

Regidor Clements patted John's arm proudly, "You did a fine job!" Clements looked at the man on his right. "Martin, the boys elected you captain of our Gonzales volunteers. You take over and tell us what to do."

Captain Albert Martin faced the group and said, "Boys, with most of our men away from Gonzales seein' to their families, that leaves about eighteen of us here to defend our homes. Be sure your guns are loaded. Let's go." The captain and his band headed for the river. Jacob Darst, Thomas Miller, Joseph Clements, John Sowell, Valentine Bennett, Thomas Jackson, and the others, realized the future of Gonzales rested in their hands.

Nearing the Guadalupe, they could see the Mexican officer and his dragoons on the opposite bank. John resumed his place on the tree limb to watch.

"Just look," Martin mumbled under his breath.

8

"Bet there's a hundred and fifty or more dragoons with that lieutenant over there. Seems to me Ugartechea's expectin' trouble — sendin' so many."

Darst chuckled softly, "Maybe we'd better use Injun tactics and make them think there's a bunch of us."

"Good idea! Miller, you, Sowell, and Davis weave in among the trees on my right. Darst, you and Bennet go with Turner on the left. Clements, you and Williams move in among those bushes over there, but keep your guns in sight." Martin waited until they were in position before he shouted, "Lieutenant, can I help you?"

The Mexican officer nodded. "*Señor*, I, Francisco Castañeda, have a message from Colonel Ugartechea for your *alcalde*. Are you the *alcalde*?"

"No. Andrew Ponton is the mayor, and he's not here. I'm Captain Albert Martin."

"Then, *señor*, I will give the message to you, but the river is too high for my rider to cross. Send the ferry for him."

Martin frowned, muttering, "Dickinson, do you think that's wise?"

"Nope, I don't. Tell him to swim it."

The lieutenant was not happy with that idea, but one of his men swam over with the message demanding the return of the cannon. Martin read it slowly before giving his answer. Martin refused to surrender the weapon on the grounds he had no authority to do so.

"*Señor*," the officer's voice was angry, "I demand to see *Alcalde* Ponton — at once!"

Martin informed him he would have to wait for the mayor since he was away. It seemed there was nothing for the Mexican lieutenant to do but set up camp and wait. From the number of men zigzagging back and forth among the trees, the officer was sure there were too many Texans for his dragoons to attempt to cross the river: Martin's Indian trick had worked!

The next morning Clements yawned, rubbed his eyes sleepily, and exclaimed, "Martin, we did it! We've kept them over there all night!"

"We sure did. I just hope Matthew Caldwell's made good use of the time and alerted the others."

Darst rubbed his chin and studied the camp in the distance. "I do too. We may need all the help we can get. Looks like that lieutenant is gettin' kinda edgy."

"Ya could be right, Darst. Wonder if we ought to change our tactics with him? Clements, as *regidor* or councilman, you are next in command to Ponton with civil problems. Why not talk to him this time?"

"I'll try," Clements replied softly before raising his voice to yell, "can you hear me? Am I speaking loud enough?"

"*Si, señor,* I can hear you. I am Lieutenant Francisco Castañeda. Are you the *alcalde* of Gonzales?"

"No, I am Joseph Clements — the *regidor.*"

The lieutenant's tone was rather condescending when he said, "Only the *regidor*? An assistant? Where is the *alcalde*? I demand to see him, where is he?"

"*Alcalde* Ponton is away. He will not be back until later," Clements replied.

"I see." The officer appeared to be deciding on his next move as he paced back and forth. Finally, he stopped and gazed at the opposite bank. "One of my men swam your river with a message. Did you read it?"

"We did."

"Then, *señor,* you know Colonel Domingo Ugartechea has demanded the return of that cannon! He sent us with orders to take it back with us. What is your delay?"

Clements spoke slowly as he explained, "I told you, sir, the *alcalde* is away. You know government regulations. The *alcalde* is spokesman for the people of Gonzales. I have no real authority to take action."

"So?"

"So I will promise we'll do something by four o'clock this afternoon if Ponton has not returned. That is the best I can do."

The distance between them prevented Clements from seeing Castañeda straighten his shoulders and clench his fist. "Very well, *regidor.* I can only assume a few hours will not matter. Perhaps my men will welcome this extra time. I do not!"

"I will return at four o'clock. I give you my word." In a lower tone, Clements spoke to Martin. "Captain, I'll be back like I said, but you stay here with the boys and keep an eye on them." With those words he was gone.

The Texans spread out along the bank. Some leaned against the trees, and others sprawled lazily upon the ground to watch the Mexican soldiers. Others continued to weave in and out among the trees. John yawned and adjusted his legs to a more comfortable position on the tree limb.

Jacob Darst muttered under his breath, "Hope Clements was right, and that we'll get help once Caldwell spreads the word to the others. The longer we can stall the better. I hope my wife and Sarah

11

DeWitt and the other women were right decidin' they'd be safer in town."

"The womenfolk are just another reason for us to watch so the soldiers don't try to ford the river." Dickinson replied. "They'd be fools to try with our guns in full view."

Jesse McCoy patted the barrel of his musket and grunted, "I sure do wish they'd try! My finger's just itchin' to pull this trigger."

"McCoy," Martin's voice sounded flat, "don't you dare! We're here to guard the river, not start a war! There's to be no shooting — not yet."

"Humph! I know that, Martin. Reckon my feelin's about Texas are deeper than the rest of yours. After all, my folks were some of the first ones here. That makes my Texas roots purty deep." McCoy wrinkled his nose to squint one eye in his usual fashion. "It's 'bout time we had some changes. With or without a fight!"

The minutes ticked into hours for the men guarding the river. Meanwhile the women and children found safety and the village's Paul Revere was riding from settlement to settlement. Matthew Caldwell's message about the demands of the Mexican soldiers brought results. The settlers quickly responded to the call for help at Gonzales. Before the afternoon was over, Clements was welcoming those who rode into town. Singly and in groups they came, until the number of volunteers swelled to over one hundred. Still, they kept coming.

Clement's spirits were high when he returned to keep his appointment. The Texans now outnumbered the Mexican soldiers!

Lieutenant Castañeda was waiting. "*Señor,*" he

called. "Why not cross over to this side so I can see you better?"

"What do you think, Martin?" the councilman whispered.

"I think it's a trick, Clements," the captain replied. "You had better stay here."

"That is my feeling, too." Clements cleared his throat and shouted back, "Lieutenant, I can see and hear you from here."

"Very well, *regidor*. Where is *Alcalde* Ponton?" His tone left little doubt that Castañeda was displeased at the turn of events.

Clements replied flatly, "Ponton has not returned."

"*Amigo!* Perhaps I did not make myself clear." The speaker's eyes flashed with anger. "I — Lieutenant Francisco Cantañeda — under orders from Colonel Domingo Ugartechea of the Army of Mexico, do hereby demand the return of OUR cannon!"

The Texans tightened their grips on their guns.

"Who says it's their cannon?" Kellogg's scowl of contempt changed to a grin as he added, "Reckon he'd like to come and get it?"

Darst snorted softly, "I wish they'd try!"

"Lieutenant Castañeda," Clements called, "in the absence of the *alcalde*, it has fallen to my lot to reply to your demand." The *regidor* unrolled a paper and began to read the message he had written:

> Therefore my reply reduces itself to this. I can not, nor do I desire, to deliver up the cannon . . . and only through force will we yield. We are few in number, nevertheless we are contending for what we believe to be just principles.

13

He stopped. A mockingbird's chirp broke the tense silence. The Texans scarcely breathed.

Finally, the officer spoke. *"Regidor,"* he hissed the word. "Have you forgotten that cannon was given as a favor to help your settlement?"

Clements made no reply. Instead, he reread his message.

Another hush followed. From his haven high in the tree, John watched Castañeda clench his fist in anger and kick the dirt with the toe of his boot. That action apparently helped him change his mind because when he spoke it was in a different tone.

"Señor," the man's bravado had turned to a plea. "You have no right to retain the cannon. My orders are to return with it. I have no other instructions. In fact, we are not prepared to meet with opposition."

Clements sighed with relief, straightened his shoulders and declared boldly, "That's your problem! You have our answer." Turning on his heel, he spoke to Martin. "Some of the boys will stay here and guard the river with you. The rest will come with me. We'll plan our next move."

Without a backward look, Joseph Clements started for the square with some of the men. John walked close behind.

On the opposite side of the Guadalupe, the 150 Mexican soldiers realized their leader was not pleased by Clement's actions. He stormed in their direction with his hands behind his back and his eyes fixed on the ground. Lieutenant Castañeda had to admit he had met defeat for the moment. He swore he would correct the situation — one way or another.

John Gaston marveled at the change. Yesterday

there had been an air of nervousness and apprehension. Today, the first of October, with the arrival of armed volunteers from the other settlements, the men of Gonzales were feeling confident. They were boasting they could drive Castañeda's soldiers away from Gonzales. After much discussion, they selected two of the new volunteers to be in charge.

Regidor Clements stood up and said, "Men, you have chosen John Moore and J. E. Wallace as your officers. Moore will serve as colonel and Wallace as lieutenant colonel. Will you two please step forward?" He moved aside for them.

The 150 or so Texans squatting around the town's square waited expectantly. John Moore looked from man to man while he talked. "The first thing we must do is unearth that cannon. I understand it's buried in the ground. Is that correct?" He glanced in Clement's direction and waited.

With a nod the *regidor* replied, "That's right. It's over in George Davis's peach orchard."

"Who put it there?"

Darst spoke up. "I did, sir, along with some of the others."

"Fine. How about digging it up?"

A devilish grin spread over Darst's face. "Be glad to, sir, if we're gonna use it. Come on, Sowell, we've work to do." They headed for the orchard on the run.

"Now," Moore continued, "we'll need wheels so we can mount that cannon."

Valentine Bennet stepped forward. "Don't worry about wheels, sir. I'll get those."

"Good! Next, we'll need a blacksmith to make ammunition for that weapon. Where is a blacksmith?"

15

"Here I am," Dickinson declared. "And Sowell and Chisholm are blacksmiths."

"Any idea what you can use to make shot?" the colonel asked.

"Well," Dickinson stroked his chin thoughtfully, "there's some chain in the shop. We'll try that."

"What kind of cannonballs can you make out of chain? We —" Thomas Miller did not get to finish.

"Somebody's comin'!" John Gaston shouted.

A deep voice questioned, "Who is it?"

"Looks like — " John stopped. "It's okay! It's Galba and Ben Fuqua!"

"What's wrong, Benjamin?" Clements demanded when the two ran through the crowd.

"It's that Castañeda! He's headin' upstream!" Benjamin paused long enough to catch his breath. "Captain Martin thinks he's movin' up to Ezekiel William's place."

"That's right," said Galba. "The river's shallow enough up there. They can get across without much trouble."

A brief hush was broken by everyone talking at once. Colonel Moore attempted to make himself heard. Finally, he shouted, "Men! Give me your attention!" When he could be heard, he went on. "That's more like it. Now, if the Mexican soldiers have moved out, we will too, as soon as that cannon's mounted."

Someone shouted, "Now you're talkin'! Hey — " the speaker stopped to stare at the women hurrying in their direction. Sarah DeWitt reached the square with several women following her. Mrs. Dewitt went to the front of the crowd alone, and stopped in front of the colonel.

16

"Hello, ma'am," he nodded solemnly. Slipping the dilapidated hat from his head, Moore smiled. "How are you, Mrs. DeWitt."

Sarah DeWitt nodded at him, then turned and smiled at the group. "We women wanted to do our part for Gonzales. Evaline, you and Cynthia bring the flag here." She paused, waiting for her daughter and Cynthia Burns to reach her side. Evaline placed a folded bundle of material carefully into her mother's outstretched arms. "We used my daughter Naomi's wedding dress to make the flag."

"Is the flag finished?" Moore asked.

Cynthia caught one corner of the fabric, and Evaline another as Sarah proudly unfurled the flag. A picture of the cannon and the words COME AND TAKE IT were printed in black on the white background.

The colonel's face lighted up with pleasure. "Thank you, ladies. You've made a mighty fine flag! We will be proud to place it over the cannon when we march to meet the enemy. Won't we, men?"

A mighty roar of approval went up from the group. Their cheer faded and, to their surprise, a strange noise took its place.

He-e-e Haw! He-e-e Haw!

"Well, I'll be," Ezekiel Williams yelled. "That's a mule! I'd knowed that sound anywhere!"

Ben Fuqua slapped his leg and laughed. "Well, you're right about the sound, Ezekiel! Look there — a white mule!"

Dickinson stared from the lop-eared animal to the man who had been riding it. "He must be that Methodist preacher I've heard about. I understand he rides a white mule."

Somehow the rider did not look like a preacher with his brown hair erupting in all directions from beneath the battered hat. The soiled buckskin pants he wore were stiff, and the sleeves of his threadbare homespun shirt reached almost to his elbows. The man's soft brown eyes fairly danced, and a grin spread across his bearded face. In spite of his outward appearance, the group knew he was a preacher when he opened his mouth to speak. His voice was gentle and kind. "That's me! Folks call me W. P. Smith. I heard Gonzales is expectin' trouble. Me and old Flick — that's my mule over there — figured we'd join you, if you wanted us."

Ben Fuqua was the first to find his voice. "Ya betcha, parson! We could truly use some help from above."

The others agreed.

It was late afternoon when, with the cannon mounted on the cart at the front of the group, they prepared to move out. The flag atop the weapon waved proudly in the breeze.

"Martin, how far is it to this place where you think Castañeda's heading?" the colonel questioned.

Captain Martin thought for a moment and then answered, "Oh, I reckon it's about seven miles, sir. Of course, you know there's always a chance that Castañeda might get reinforcements."

"That's a chance we have to take," Colonel Moore replied. His command was loud and clear as he shouted, "All right, let's march!"

With that, the excited Texans headed out. Fifty horsemen were soon in the lead, followed by the parson's white mule and the cart with the cannon. Those afoot brought up the rear.

The light of day was fading when they reached the spot where the ferry boats were hidden. The cart with the cannon was quickly loaded onto one ferry.

18

Another carried those who were walking while the riders rode their swimming horses through the water and up to the opposite bank.

The colonel announced, "Pass the word along: soon as everybody's across we'll start a fire and rest. Warn the men to keep the racket down."

After a fire was started, the men watched Darst place a blackened pot on the glowing coals.

With a chuckle he explained, "That's my wife's idea! She figured we'd need some coffee before this night's over."

"She's right," Miller nodded. "I'll give you a new hat for a cup."

Darst's brown eyes twinkled as he spoke, "I guess that's a fair trade. Say, if you are a preacher, Smith, ya got your *Bible* with ya?"

"Surely do! I never go nowhere without it."

"I'll give a cup of coffee to hear ya read. I never learned letters myself. Back in Tennessee, there weren't many schools on the frontier." There was a trace of sadness in Darst's voice when he mentioned Tennessee and the old days.

"I can't read either," someone muttered hoarsely.

Others, too, said they would enjoy hearing the preacher. They pleaded with the preacher to read from his Book. He finally agreed to do so.

"Now," Smith began as he stepped upon a dead tree stump. "You recall when we first came to Texas we swore to be good citizens of Mexico, and Catholics? Since I am not a priest, I've had no chance to preach. I'm kinda rusty."

Dickinson smiled and said, "Don't worry about that. We have heard no preaching for a long time, so we won't know the difference!"

The others nodded.

With that, Smith flipped the pages of his *Bible* until he came to I Samuel. With a nervous cough, he said, "You have all heard the story about the giant, Goliath? Nobody had been able to kill that bully until David come along. That lad stepped up with a smooth stone and his sling, and killed him dead! The forty-fifth verse says:

Then said David to the Philistine, Thou comest to me with a sword, and with a spear, and with a shield; but I come to thee in the name of the Lord of hosts, the God of the armies of Israel.

Smith closed the Book and looked at the men seated at his feet. "I believe this Mexican army we're gonna face is like that giant. They've better guns and trainin', but remember, David needed just a little old stone in a sling to kill that giant in the name of the Lord.

"Now, those Philistines were pushin' David's folks around like old Santa Anna's pushin' us around. And we don't like the shoving, do we? As I recall, our forefathers fought that Revolution because the English were pushin' them round. Haven't we got the blood of our ancestors in us?"

Heads nodded yes.

"It is just not right for this Mexican feller to demand that," he glanced at the cannon while he talked. "Our cannon is not very big — but what it stands for is pretty big! It stands for bravery. The kind you feel when you're willin' to fight a feller twice your size. It stands for honor. Like standin' up for what's right — regardless of the cost. And . . . it stands for pride. Like when a job's well done. In fact, you might say that cannon represents things we hold dear — like family, home and . . . and country. I heard someone say 'Great will be the influence resulting from the effort we're about to make!' "

"And what does <u>that</u> mean?" Darst demanded.

Smith chuckled softly. "Don't rightly know. Could mean always do your best. Or, to put it another way, us refusin' to give up that cannon may seem a little thing, but it just might be mighty big to Texas. Men, let's not forget, David didn't kill that giant by himself. He had help and we need help. Let's bow our heads and ask for it.

Lord, you helped David whop old Goliath. We're prayin' for your help in whatever we're gonna face. We're asking, too, for your blessing and protection on us. Amen.

A wolf howled in the distance. The parson went on. "Texas is real important to me. In fact, I'm reminded of a man named Patrick Henry who said, 'Give me liberty or give me death!' I'm willin' to die, if need be, for Texas and that cannon. How about all of you?" With that thought provoking question, Parson Smith stepped into the shadows.

Colonel Moore took his place. "Thank you, reverend, for that inspiring message. It will be one we'll remember." The colonel looked at one of the men and said, "I understand you're Ezekiel Williams."

"That's me."

"Well, seeing it's dark and we're heading for your place, maybe you'd better lead us."

And so it was that Ezekiel directed the Texans up the river. Fog and the moonless night prevented Castañeda's patrols from seeing the Texans silently move into position opposite the Mexican force.

21

When the fog began to lift the next morning, the sleepy-eyed Mexican dragoons made a startling discovery: the cannon they had come to get was aimed at them! So were some 160 rifles and muskets.

In his excitement, Darst accidentally fired his musket. That, in turn, caused the Texans to open fire. Castañeda's bewildered men fell back as the Texans inched forward.

"Stop!" Colonel Moore shouted. "There's a white flag. The lieutenant's coming this way. Hold your fire, boys! I'll see what he wants."

The two men advanced to within speaking distance. Castañeda shouted angrily, "*Senōr!* How dare you fire on us? Are you *loco?*"

"Hardly! That's our response to your demand to the return of our cannon."

Castañeda shook his fist at him, growling, "But, *señor,* I have orders from Colonel Ugartechea of the Army of Mexico. He is under the command of the *Presidente* General Santa Anna!"

Moore selected his words with care as he explained the Texans were determined to fight for their rights as stated in the Constitution of 1824. He went on to say that Santa Anna appeared to be opposing the Constitution and the laws of Mexico. The colonel then suggested that the lieutenant either surrender his troops or join up with the Texans in their fight against Santa Anna.

"What? How dare you?" the man's dark eyes flashed with rage. "I, Francisco Castañeda, am a loyal citizen of Mexico. I obey orders. I demand the surrender of that cannon!"

The colonel spit out his words, "Then come and take it!"

"But . . . but," the officer's face reddened as he

stammered, "I have no orders to fight!" He eyed the cannon along with the rugged frontiersmen who glared at him. He looked back at his own troops. "In fact, I do not think my men are prepared to fight."

"You should have thought of that!" Moore turned on his heel and shouted, "Men, fire on the count of three." The Mexican lieutenant wasted no time returning to his group.

On the count of three, the Texans again opened fire. This time the Mexican soldiers had no thought of fighting. Instead, they turned and fled in the direction of San Antonio. Their leader was not far behind them.

"Yip-eee-e!" John Gaston shouted from his perch in a tree. "They're headin' through Ezekiel's watermelons as fast as they can go!"

"What?" Ezekiel Williams ran for his field and stopped short. He looked in horror at what the enemy had done. "Them critters done ruined all my watermelons! Shoot the cannon again, colonel, don't let 'em get away!"

The colonel lit the fuse. The cannon's noise vibrated with such force that Gaston tumbled from his perch. Everyone laughed and shouted at once.

"Dadburn! What a racket! Bet that cannon's shot'll be heard halfway round the world." Williams shouted with excitement above the sound and confusion.

Albert Martin watched the others dancing around with joy and smiled. But after a few minutes he sighed thoughtfully. It was true they had saved their cannon, but what would happen now? What would Santa Anna do next?

The Gathering Clouds

The thrill of victory brought life to Gonzales. Susanna Dickinson, Elizabeth George, and others hurried back home after hiding from the threat of attack. Men from other settlements continued to arrive to offer their assistance.

Everyone talked about Castañeda's unwillingness to "come and take it." But the excitement of their victory was short-lived. On October 6, they learned Colonel Ugartechea himself was heading for Gonzales, with 500 men to seize the cannon. Shortly after midnight the men in Gonzales sent a message to one of the most respected citizens of Texas, Stephen Austin. They asked him to come to their aide and to bring powder and lead with him.

While they waited for Austin's reply, the men set up camp in Eli Mitchell's cornfield and discussed possible solutions to the situation. They agreed it would be best to carry the fight to San Antonio, in hope of avoiding what could become a battleground in Gonzales. Austin arrived a few days later. When the volunteers elected him commander-in-chief, Austin set about to organize the soldier volunteers into companies. He selected Almeron Dickinson to be the officer in charge of the cannon.

Once the assignments were made, Austin called the group together to make a speech. "You have no doubt heard by now that Santa Anna considers all who oppose him to be traitors. Retreat is now impossible, we must go forward to victory or die the death of traitors. I will wear myself out by inches rather than submit to Santa Anna's rule." Austin's face was grim and solemn. It was common knowledge he had gone to Mexico to talk of rights for Texas and had been thrown into prison. At the age of forty-two, Austin's two-year imprisonment had left him sickly, and would bring about his death in less than a year. Austin's one thought was freedom for Texas.

October 13 dawned bright and crisp. The adventurous ragtag army of Texans prepared to march out of Gonzales toward San Antonio. They wore a strange array of clothing and carried a variety of firearms from muskets to rifles and squirrel guns. The citizens felt sure of victory, with men like Ben Milam and Jim Bowie on their side. Everyone had a deep respect for Jim Bowie's ability. His fights with his Bowie knife had made him famous. They knew, too, of Milam's courage. Milam's men had been greatly outnumbered by the Mexican soldiers when they had captured the Mexican fort at Goliad a few days earlier. Too, they felt certain of success with Stephen Austin as their commander. With those facts it was no wonder their spirits were high.

Finally, the command was given, "Move out, men!"

Excitement filled the air. Women and children waved and shouted as Austin led the volunteers down the street. Almeron Dickinson and the "Come and Take It Cannon," with it's flag flying high, brought up the rear. Some rode mules with long ears, others rode big farm horses or smaller Spanish ponies.

The town faded in the distance as they rode on. Houses became fewer and fewer in number. The men had not gone far when they discovered the ox-drawn cart hampered their progress. Movement was extremely slow.

Hour after hour, mile after mile, they plodded along. The sun rose higher and higher as the day wore on. They rode up hills and down gulleys, past underbrush and around cactus. It was late when they made camp for the night. After that first day, one day was like another. With the passing of time, they began to wonder about the fate of the poorly constructed cart. It had not been designed for such a trip. The wheels squeaked noisily, zigzagging crazily over the rough, uneven road. They were approaching Sandy Creek when Dickinson realized something was the matter. Suddenly, like a dying man's last gasps, the cart stopped. The axle had broken! Dickinson was unable to prevent the two wheels from collapsing in opposite directions. The cannon seemed to hang in midair for one brief moment, then crashed to the ground.

Once Dickinson found his voice, he shouted, "Stop!"

All eyes turned. The volunteer soldiers from Gonzales could only stare at their noble six-pounder. What could they say? The axle of the cart was broken beyond repair. It would be impossible to move the weapon any farther without a cart. There seemed nothing to do but abandon the cannon and move on. And they did, but their spirits were dampened, knowing they had forsaken the trusty six-pounder that had started their fight for Texas freedom.

It was sometime later when someone shouted, "Ain't much further. There's Espada!"

The old church on the outskirts of town was one of five missions in San Antonio. While the others stopped to rest, Jim Bowie and James Fannin took a company of ninety men to scout the area for a campsite.

Darkness was falling when they spied the twin towers of Mission Concepción in the distance. Like Espada, the one hundred-year-old church had long since been deserted, but it would offer them protection from the cold mist.

They awoke the next morning to find themselves surrounded by a force of 400 Mexican cavalrymen.

After a brief discussion with Fannin, Bowie took command. "Prepare for attack. Keep under cover, we haven't a man to spare."

The battle lasted about thirty minutes. It left one Texan dead but the Mexicans lost sixty. A large number of the enemy lay wounded or dying. As the gunsmoke cleared, the main Texas Army arrived. The Mexican troops fled.

Austin's group joined Bowie's men at Concepción and cheered at the news of another victory. But Austin reminded them their one and only cannon was back by Sandy Creek, and they would need heavy artillery to face the Mexican's cannons. Besides that, he reminded them their ammunition was getting low. So, instead of marching to face General Cos's soldiers, the Texans made camp to wait — and wait they did.

October ended. November came and went. The volunteers grew weary with waiting; many returned home. Finally, on December 5, Ben Milam led a band of Texans into San Antonio to fight. Five days later Cos and Ugartechea surrendered. The general agreed to take the troops back across the Rio Grande to Mexico, and never return to Texas.

The Texans had won in spite of staggering odds against them and had lost only two men in the battle. One was Ben Milam. The enemy suffered a number of casualties with 150 dead and many wounded.

Once more the settlers were jubilant: they had defeated the Mexican army and would be home for Christmas. Life in Texas could settle back to normal — or so they thought.

"What a feast, Missus King. Thanks fer invitin' me to share William's turkey and honey." John Gaston patted his stomach happily. "I'm full as a tick!"

William King groaned, "Me too! But, John, you're the one who found the bee tree. I only smoked out the bees so we could get the honey. Benjamin and Galba shot the turkey. Ma's cookin' did the rest!" The teenager looked from his two friends, Galba and John, to Benjamin Fuqua, his brother-in-law. Benjamin's young wife was Williams's older sister, Nancy.

"Well, I reckon all of you young folk did your part. That's a meal fit for any King." John King's eyes twinkled as he gazed from his nine children to his wife, Parmelia. What more could a man ask out of life than a family, a home, and friends. John King stretched and smiled contentedly.

The fire in the huge fireplace warmed the room

and sent an elusive fragrance of wood that mingled with that from leafy boughs decorating the mantle. The burning candles on the long table cast soft shadows on the ceiling. The largest piece of furniture was the bed in the corner. In the middle of it was Nancy and Benjamin's only baby, little Mary.

John King sighed. "You know I'm mighty proud of this place. We're lucky to have so much. Benjamin, I'm especially proud Nancy's got a fine husband like you." His voice softened. "And, of course, that grandbaby over there is the joy of our life."

Benjamin chuckled. "I'm always tellin' Galba I couldn't have married into a better family, not even back in Virginia. Galba and me — we've felt like part of the King family ever since you let us call you Ma and Pa. I tease Nancy and say I keep her because of you all. You know, since Silas died last year, Galba's looked to me for advice. We both look to you and Nancy's mother."

"Ben, sometimes I think my folks love you more than me," Nancy grumbled. "Now, before you men start talkin', I'm gonna say somethin'. I'm sick to death with talk of politics and war, so don't talk about it. This is Christmas, a time to celebrate!"

Milly King shook her finger in her husband's direction. "Nancy's right, John. No talk of Santa Anna, you hear?"

"All right, if you say so," Pa grumbled.

"Well, Pa, if ya can't talk about fightin'," the youngest King's eyes sparkled, "you can tell us a story about the olden days. Would you?"

The family echoed the request. Stories were a rare treat they all enjoyed.

John King chuckled softly and leaned back in his chair to get comfortable. With so many mouths

29

to feed, it wasn't often he took time for a story. By the end of a day he was usually too tired to think of anything. "What would you like to hear?"

"About comin' to Texas!"

"James, you've heard the story a hundred times!"

"I know — but tell it again!"

"Very well. Back in eighteen thirty when Milly and I came to Texas, you were five, James."

"Well, I'm ten now!

"Boy, you were just a little shaver when Green DeWitt brought us from South Carolina. Ben, I remember the day you and Galba's father joined our group."

"I do too. Our brother Ephraim had settled on the Brazos River, but my other brother, Silas, wanted to be in DeWitt's Colony. Silas needed me because Galba was nine when their mother died, and there were six children! Silas and me took turns bein' ma and pa to a passel of children! I'll never forget the trip to Gonzales, with all those youngsters!"

Milly's brows wrinkled in a frown, "I doubt any of us will!"

Pa King continued, "Once we got here, most folks wanted to settle close to town, but we wanted elbow room. So did your dad, Galba. We claimed this land out from town, with our nearest neighbor Silas — and he was two miles away! I've not been sorry we settled out here, have you, Milly?"

The large woman shook her head slowly as she replied, "No, I can't say I have. Not even when we worked from sunup to sundown without time to see another soul. For awhile, work here was never done!"

"True. I used to wonder if we'd ever get all those

30

trees chopped and uprooted, but we finally did. Of course, with so many rocks and stumps, at first we had to work hard to till the land. You all remember helpin' me?"

Heads nodded. They remembered. It had been hard labor.

With a thoughtful expression on his face, William glanced around. "I can remember helpin' ya build this cabin. Course, one room never was big enough fer all us Kings. The girls were happy to get their own cabin."

"So was Ma," Nancy said with a smile.

James lifted his eyes to the attic and scratched his head. "I'll never forget the first night we slept up there. I always hated sleepin' on the dirt floor even if it was on a pallet."

"Maybe so, boy," his father said, "but that dirt floor was smooth as butter from us Kings stompin' it down. This puncheon floor is something else. I wonder if the wood splinters will ever get smooth? I doubt it." He eyed a rough spot in the floor, then went on. "One thing I'll always remember about that first year was the heat. The heat was awful! Even though your Ma has always been nervous about wild animals, that summer we slept under the stars. Animals, insects, and all were better than the heat in here."

"It was like an oven in this house before you cut out those windows, that's for sure!" his wife exclaimed.

"I can still see you cookin' outdoors, Milly."

His wife's eyes flashed as she snapped, "Humph! So can I! I was always cookin' and washin' with so many Kings to feed! And dirt! I never saw

31

such dirt! Seemed the girls and I were forever boilin' water and washin' clothes!"

"And Ma," Nancy declared, "things are the same now I'm married. Benjamin and Galba are always dirty!" She wrinkled her nose mischieviously, glancing in Galba's direction. "He's almost as messy as William. Reckon it's because they're boys and don't know better?"

"No, they're just growin' boys and can't help it." Pa King added, "Climbin' trees for honey and trampin' through the mud to shoot a wild turkey is dirty work, girl. But just look at the meal it brought us."

In spite of herself Nancy laughed at her brother's know-it-all expression and muttered, "Maybe so, Pa, maybe so."

December came to a close. With their defeat of General Cos, the volunteers left San Antonio to be home in time for the holidays. Most of the Texans felt Mexico would now respect their rights. At first, no one wanted to listen to General Sam Houston's warnings that Santa Anna might cause them trouble again. Texans began the new year of 1836, dreaming of a better year to come. With the news Stephen Austin had gone to the States to raise money and enlist more recruits for the Texas army, an uneasy feeling filled the air.

In Gonzales, Almeron Dickinson did little to calm those fears. He announced he was returning to the Alamo to rejoin those who had stayed behind. His wife, Susanna, and their child were going with him. Sarah DeWitt and others attempted to change Susanna's mind.

Her answer was, "My place is with my husband. If he's going, Angelina and I are going, too." No amount of talking could convince the nineteen-year-old Susanna to stay behind.

Meanwhile, the Fuqua kinsmen had sorrow of their own.

One night Galba dreamed Nancy was screaming at him, "Galba, get Pa — Benjamin's bad sick. Hurry, boy, hurry!"

Suddenly Galba realized it was not a dream: Nancy was shaking him and screaming in his ear. Ben was sick! Galba jumped into his clothes and dashed out of the house to his pony with no thought of saddle or bridle. Like a phantom rider in the night, he raced for help. Pa King lost no time rallying to his cry. But, in spite of their haste, they found Nancy huddled quietly beside her husband's bed. Benjamin Fuqua was dead.

The dazed teenager could only stare in disbelief. He imagined he heard his uncle say again, "Do your best, Galba. Like a flower, life wilts and fades. Death is a breath away."

But how could death come so quickly — without warning? First to his mother when he was nine. Then his father was gone, and now Benjamin.

Galba whispered, "If I start crying, it will be hard to stop. I've got to be strong." He didn't feel strong. He felt like a sixteen-year-old who had lost his friend, the best uncle a boy ever had.

Pa King took his daughter and Galba in his arms. Their tears did not wash away the hurt but they eased the sorrow.

The days that followed were a blur. Yet, somehow life went on.

Everyone talked of Santa Anna's army of thousands that was preparing for an all-out attack. Sam Houston's warning echoed through the settlements: "It seems Santa Anna's going to march to San Antonio and on through Texas! Prepare to fight!"

The Alamo

<u>War? Freedom?</u>

Those words were repeated over and over. Rumors, true and false, flew back and forth. The citizens grew more nervous. January ended, February brought rain along with the bitter cold.

To pass the time, the men of Gonzales took to meeting at Winslow Turner's Inn. Galba Fuqua and John Gaston and their friends crowded in to listen to the talk. Like most boys their age, they yearned for excitement and adventure. Talk of war fired their imagination and desire to fight.

One evening William Dearduff remarked, "Do you all remember last month when Colonel Neill was commander of the Alamo, and how he asked for men and supplies?"

"I do!" James George spoke up. "Since General Houston's in charge of the whole army, he answered Neill's request by sendin' Jim Bowie with thirty men. They were carryin' orders to blow up the Alamo, but nobody obeyed that order!"

Turner said, "That's right. Then Neill turned his command of the Alamo over to Jim Bowie and Colonel Travis and he went home."

34

"Never did understand that," Johnny Kellogg remarked. "Everybody in Texas knows Bowie's a born leader!"

"What you say's true, Kellogg. But Bowie's been different since his wife and children died from cholera. Some say he's a sick man. On the other hand, I understand this William Travis's a real capable fellow," George Kimball exclaimed. "He ought to be able to handle things."

Darst scratched his beard thoughtfully as he said, "If Santa Anna does attack, Travis will need more men. Didn't he send James Bonham to Goliad with a message to Colonel Fannin askin' for supplies?"

"Yep, but far as I know, Fannin didn't send any. It's a fact Fannin's got provisions and four hundred men in Goliad right now!" Kellogg grumbled.

Turner nodded his head, "And Travis needs them! Even with Almeron Dickinson and Marcus Sowell and the others from Gonzales, there won't be enough men to hold the Alamo for long."

"Dr. Amos Pollard and Andrew Duvalt are there too," Dearduff said.

"It'd take more than two hundred men to defend the Alamo. Why, it covers three acres and was never built for a fort in the first place! I understand the south wall's weak, and the north wall has a break." Kimball stared at the fire with a serious look on his face.

James George spoke up, "I thought those rock walls were eight feet high and three feet wide."

"Those walls are also a hundred years old. Santa Anna's supposed to have heavy artillery and cannons. And thousands of Mexican soldiers," Kimball replied.

With that unpleasant thought the meeting came to an end.

Night after night, the men talked and waited, wondering what would happen next.

Tension mounted, nothing happened. One day was like another until the evening of February 24, when John William Smith and Dr. John Sutherland rode into Gonzales. A crowd gathered quickly to hear the news from Colonel Travis.

"The Alamo's under attack! Santa Anna has reached San Antonio!"

"Thousands of Mexican soldiers were pouring in yesterday when Doctor Sutherland and I left."

"Colonel Travis sent this message," the doctor unfolded the letter and began to read:

> The enemy in large force is in sight. We have 150 men and are determined to defend the Alamo to the last. Give us assistance.

Sutherland looked from one to another as he said, "Travis needs your help — so does Texas. If we're to get freedom, General Houston needs time to recruit more men. Numbers of our Mexican friends agree we must hold the Alamo as long as we can."

Smith nodded his head. "Many *Tejanos* or Texas-born Mexicans are afraid because Santa Anna's become a dictator. He has made many enemies among his own people."

Rubbing his leg, Sutherland remarked, "I hurt this yesterday. But with men like Antonio Fuentes, Juan Seguin, Forbidio Losoya, and Antonio Cruz on our side, I can stand a little pain." In spite of his words the doctor looked exhausted.

As one of the leaders of the Gonzales volunteers,

Kimball spoke up. "Men, it's been a long day for these two. You go home now. Get a good night's sleep, then make your decision. If you decide to join me, gather up guns, food, blankets and ammunition. Be prepared to leave on a moment's notice once we hear from Fannin. Until then, good night."

Everyone headed home in silence. In several houses, couples talked late that night. Some of the men found sleep impossible. Others, like John Gaston, were thoughtful.

At the Davis's breakfast table next morning John cleared his throat and said, "Pa, you're the only dad I've ever known since my own died when I was little. You always said that size doesn't matter, it's how I set my sights. Didn't I set my mind on bein' the best tree climber in town? And didn't Clements let me be sentry to watch for Castañeda?"

George Davis nodded. "Your ma and me were mighty proud of you. Weren't we, Rebecca?"

"Mighty proud."

"What I'm tryin' to say is I'm goin' to the Alamo!" the boy blurted out the words.

His parents were stunned. The only sound in the room came from the hiss of the burning logs in the fireplace.

Finally, Gaston broke the spell. "It's like this. I've always dreamed of bein' big and doin' something important." He stared at the floor. "I figure helpin' somebody in need's the next best thing to bein' big."

His mother spoke up. "John Gaston! You're just a boy. What can you do?"

"Ma, Colonel Travis didn't say a thing about size or age. He's just askin' for help! I think Galba will be going, too. You wait and see."

Gaston was right about Galba.

37

A few miles away at the Fuquas', Galba made the speech he had rehearsed during the night. "Nancy, my mind's made up — I'm goin'! Your folks will let you stay with them while I'm gone."

"But, Galba —"

"No! It's settled! No need talkin'. Uncle Ben'd go if he was here, but he's not here. So I'm goin' in his place . . . and in pa's place." Galba's tone softened. "Nancy, it's like Ben is right here, whisperin' in my ear. 'Do your best each day for like the withered flower, life fades away.' Don't ya see, Nancy? I gotta go — for Ben."

Nancy knew he was pleading for her to understand. She sensed the boy's overwhelming desire to be a man, and she chose her words with care. "In my heart I know you must go, Galba. I've always known war was coming but it doesn't make it any easier. Fighting is never easy. Pa was a colonel in the War of 1812. He'll probably wanta go along, too." She tried to smile through the tears, "All right, Galba, go . . . and do your best."

An impish twinkle lighted his eyes, "Don't worry. Santa Anna will hear from me!"

Down the road Mary Millsaps declared, "Isaac, something's botherin' ya. Ya rolled and tossed all night. What is it?"

Isaac's shoulders slumped, his eyes were troubled. He studied each member of his family and shook his head. How could he think of leaving seven children and a blind wife? How?

"Speak up, man, what's wrong?"

"Nothin'," Isaac muttered.

His wife scoffed at the word. "Nothin'? We ain't been married all these years fer me not to know

38

when something's wrong. Don't ya think I know ya feel it's yer duty to go to Colonel Travis?"

"But —"

"And yer goin'! Ya hear?" Mary, of course, could not see her husband's mouth fall open in surprise. She went on, "Don't ya think I can take care of myself after havin' all these young 'uns without no help? Blind or not, Isaac Millsaps, I come from Mississippi to be a Texan."

"But —"

She shook her head. "No, let me finish. If we're Texans, we oughta fight fer what's right. Me and the children would be ashamed if ya didn't wanta go. Ya wouldn't want us to be ashamed of ya, would ya?"

"No —"

Mary's jaw was set. "Then yer goin'! That's settled. Don't ya fret about me. Ain't I got seven children to fetch and tote fer me? What could ya do they can't?"

From the expression on the children's faces, Isaac knew his wife was right. They had been trained to work and help their parents. The older boys did a man's work every day.

"So, that's settled! Start gettin' yer things together so ya can go along with the others and do yer part."

Before dawn, George Kimball crept silently out of his bed. He wanted to be alone, as he often did when he had something on his mind. Later that morning George found Prudence washing clothes by the river bank. He looked from the baby to his pretty wife, and tried to find words. Slowly he explained why he must answer Travis's desperate plea, it was his duty. George didn't want to excite her, but he explained that if Santa Anna did march through Texas

as people thought he would, they would lose everything — hat factory, house, and more. Prudence lis-
tened, and, with tear filled eyes, finally agreed he
must obey his heart. He must go to Travis's aid.

And so it was. One by one the men made their
decisions: Jesse McCoy, Dolphin Floyd, William
Dearduff and his brother-in-law James George, and
the wealthiest man in town — Thomas Miller — and
others. They all decided to answer Colonel Travis's
plea for help.

Late Friday a lone rider on a weary horse rap-
idly approached the outskirts of Gonzales. Captain
Albert Martin had ridden all day with another ur-
gent message from Travis. Martin asked himself if
they would listen to him. And Fannin? Where was
Fannin? he wondered.

Kimball saw the rider coming. A crowd began to
form around them. Martin read Travis's letter ad-
dressed "To the People of Texas and All Americans
in the World." With his mission complete, Martin
was eager to return to the Alamo without delay. But
he decided to wait until Kimball could rally his men.

It was noon the next day by the time the high-
spirited volunteers gathered in the village square. A
sharp north wind forced their families to hurry their
final farewells.

The captain of the Gonzales volunteer army,
George Kimball, raised his hand to get attention.
"Boys, I'll ride up front with Smith and Martin. Kellogg, you and Gaston come next with Cottle and
Kent behind you. The rest will follow. Floyd, you
and Millsaps bring up the rear. Be on the lookout for
others who'll join us along the way. We'll camp for
the night on the other side of John King's place.
Okay, men, let's go."

In a flurry of excitement they were off. As they passed the Davises, Sydney Kellogg, Johnny's pretty wife, and her mother, Rebecca Davis, were in front waving to the troops. The two women stood shivering in the cold until the riders disappeared from sight. With hats pulled low to face the wind, the Texans rode on.

A few miles down the road in the Kings' house, William turned to face his father. He declared firmly, "Pa, you're not goin'! It's not right for you to go. Ma and the family need you here. I've made up my mind. I'm goin' alone!"

William's mother looked at him in surprise. After a few minutes of thoughtful silence, she straightened her shoulders and said, "John, he's right. You're stayin' home! You've had your turn a fightin' in a war. Now it's William's turn."

John rubbed his beard and pondered over the problem. Finally, with a deep sigh of reluctance, he nodded his head. Early in their marriage he had learned Parmelia was usually right. If she said stay, he would stay. William would go alone.

With that settled, William said farewell to his brothers and sisters, kissed his parents and gathered his things. He was ready to join the group when they rode past. With a shout and wave to his family, William rode on with the other volunteers.

The hours and miles slipped by. The day wore on. Near dusk they stopped to make camp. After their meal, the men sat around the fire and talked until they fell asleep. With the first light of dawn, the men came to life. After a hurried breakfast, they were on the way again.

The men rode all day Sunday. The weather turned bitterly cold by Monday. Gaston's heart

41

skipped a beat when he heard the boom of cannons as they neared San Antonio. John Smith heard them too. He dashed ahead to scout the area and when he returned reported the Alamo was surrounded.

"We'll keep out of sight till Santa Anna's camp settles for the night, then we'll go in." Smith added, "If we're lucky, the Mexican sentries will be nappin' at their posts."

It was midnight when they cautiously inched their way forward. Zigzagging back and forth, they headed silently for the dark outline of the Alamo. As they drew near a bullet suddenly whizzed through the air.

"Tarnation!" one of the Texans yelled angrily. "Stop shootin'! We're friends! That critter grazed my foot!"

When the sentry heard his voice, he threw open the gate. The thirty-two riders scurried to safety before the gate slammed shut. Word of their arrival spread like wildfire around the compound. With news of reinforcements, no one thought of sleep.

A tall man wearing a coonskin cap shouted, "Let's celebrate! Someone build a big fire. We'll roast a beef. Hand me my fiddle and we'll have a tune!"

"Yepee, Davy Crockett! That's the way!" someone yelled. The courtyard exploded with excitement.

The next morning, Colonel Travis declared the first day of March a day of celebration. He rescinded his order — not to fire unless necessary because of the shortage of ammunition — and allowed the cannoneers to fire toward Santa Anna's camp.

The men stood around watching Dickinson and his helper on the church roof load their cannons. With much ado, Dickinson shouted, "Fire cannon one!" Then he paused and shouted, "Fire cannon two!"

No one breathed. All eyes turned to the west. As the men watched, one of the cannon scored a hit on the house that served as Santa Anna's headquarters. Pieces of rock and debris were hurled into the sky. The men went wild! To add to their noise, Crockett fiddled and sang a loud song. The men danced around like children. Galba joined in the fun by grabbing Kellogg and doing a jig. King and Gaston laughed and cheered them on. John McGregor, the Scotsman who had joined their cause, took his bagpipe and began to play. The unusual music brought shouts of wonder and laughter from the men.

The women and children who had taken refuge inside the old church came out to watch the celebration. Susanna Dickinson and her little daughter were among the watchers.

Suddenly, the party came to an abrupt halt. The Mexican cannons boomed! The children screamed and ran for cover. Their mothers were right behind them.

The Texans quickly returned to their posts. Dickinson took William King up to the church roof to help man the cannons. Crockett and his Tennesseans were stationed on the south wall and Kimball and Martin joined them there. The others from Gonzales took positions as riflemen wherever they were needed.

Bullets whizzed from first one direction and then another. The volunteers made each shot count, for they had none to waste. Then as suddenly as it started, the firing stopped. After a brief lull, there was another attack. Time and again the Mexican soldiers fired and loaded, fired and loaded. The distance between them prevented the short-range Mexican guns from hitting their mark. The rock walls of the old mission were not so fortunate. With the constant shelling, the weak spots grew weaker. During the periods of silence, Green Jameson's men strengthened the breaks in the walls with piles of dirt. James George and Dearduff and others packed the dirt with their hands.

During the brief lulls between attacks, the men exchanged stories. Rumor had it Fannin was on his way from Goliad with 200 or more men. It was a fact that James Bonham had ridden from the Alamo on February 27, on his second trip to Goliad. Everyone agreed that if the thirty-two men from Gonzales had gotten through the lines, Fannin could do the same. They figured Bonham should have made the ninety-mile trip in two days. That would mean reinforcements from Goliad could come at anytime.

Gaston joined the sentries on the east wall. Shivering from the sharp cold wind, they watched and waited. In the distance they could see some of the Mexican soldiers in white shirts and pants clustered around a fire. They obviously were not dressed for the freezing weather either.

That night Santa Anna's troops made sleep impossible. March 2, came and went with still no sign of Fannin. The enemy's incessant bombardment continued until midmorning on March 3. Then it stopped.

Gaston took advantage of the lull to yawn and stretch his legs. Glancing toward San Antonio he saw the bloodred flag fluttering above the church steeple. He had been told that flag meant no quarter. The flag meant that no prisoners would be taken, that all would be killed. Shuddering at the thought, Gaston turned back toward the east. Suddenly something caught his attention. Gaston glued his eyes to the spot. He saw a lone rider make his way through the thicket and underbrush.

Gaston found his voice. "Look! Over there. Somebody's comin'!"

His companions saw the horseman, too, and shouted, "Get ready to open the east gate. Somebody's coming! Looks like Bonham! There's a white cloth tied around his hat."

The rider crouched low over his horse's neck as the horse moved swiftly over the ground. The Mexican soldiers were too surprised to fire at him until it was too late. The horseman galloped through the open gate, it slammed shut behind him.

"Get word to Colonel Travis. James Bonham's back!" the sentry shouted.

"Where is Fannin?" someone yelled.

Bonham did not answer. Instead, he hurried to report to his friend William Travis. Bonham and Travis had once been schoolboy companions. He dreaded to give his message but, with a heavy sigh, he did. "Fannin's not coming!"

"Not coming?"

Sweat-soaked hat in hand, Bonham shook his head. "No, William, he's not coming. Seems he started out but their wagons broke down. They turned back to Goliad, and there they stayed."

The Colonel's blue eyes flashed with anger. "So much for Fannin! After you left, Juan Seguin rode out on the twenty-fifth. Perhaps he will hear of this and get word to General Houston. Surely someone will send us help."

Their conversation was cut short by shouts and

noise from the enemy camp. From his post on the church roof, Dickinson shouted, "Look! Reinforcements! Santa'a Anna's gettin' thousands of 'em!"

It was midnight on March 3, when John Smith prepared to ride out of the Alamo for the second time. He carried a packet of letters in his saddle bag. One was Travis's letter to Governor Smith. Travis had ended that message with a cry for help. "God and Texas — Victory or Death."

There were other letters in the packet, too. Upon Travis's suggestion, some of the men had written letters to their families. One of them was Isaac Millsaps's letter to his wife, Mary. Willis Moore, too, had scribbled a message to his family. Other men had done the same.

With a farewell nod, Smith mounted his horse. He slipped out the east gate to vanish into the night as the Texans diverted the enemy's attention in the opposite direction. He managed to get past the Mexican patrols unnoticed. With a sigh, and a quick look around to be sure he was not being followed, Smith settled comfortably in his saddle for the long ride ahead of him.

The early morning hours were filled with bursts of shooting but all the while the Mexican troops were moving closer. By dawn they were within rifle range. Most of Friday, Santa Anna's army made one attack after another. The Texans knew no peace. Days and nights without sleep were taking their toll. Both sides were tired and weary.

Santa Anna's war of nerves with constant bombardment continued throughout March 4, and on into the night. March 5, was no better until almost dusk. Suddenly the shooting stopped. There was silence — deafening silence. They waited for another attack, it did not come.

With the unexpected stillness, the women and children ventured into the courtyard. The sentries reported some of the enemy were marching out of town. The Texans heaved a sigh of relief. Crockett's men rebuilt the fires to roast a freshly killed beef. The women made tortillas from ground corn and water, while the beans were cooking. A few friends carried Jim Bowie out to get some air. Everyone was tired and hungry. They ate in silence.

Later Colonel Travis called them together to make a speech. "Men, the time has come to face the truth." He paused to choose his words. "As you know, I expected reinforcements. It seems that I was wrong. Except for the thirty-two brave men from Gonzales, no one has answered our plea. Help could not get here in time — not now. We are surrounded. So far we have not lost one man, but the enemy is preparing for a final assault. It could come at any moment."

Colonel Travis studied the faces before him: Thomas Jackson, John Flanders, William Summers, Isaac Baker, Dolphin Floyd, John Cane, and others. All good men bonded together for the cause of freedom. Travis took his sword and drew a line upon the ground. His face was solemn. "If you wish to stay and fight with me, cross this line. If you want to leave, that is all right too. I wish you luck."

Tapley Holland was the first to cross the line. The others followed him. Only Jim Bowie on his sick bed and Moses Rose were left.

"Carry me over," Bowie pleaded. And they did.

A veteran of other wars, Rose declared he had

no desire to die in Texas. Instead he vanished over the wall into the darkness of the night.

The men looked at each other and shook their heads.

"Get some sleep while you can." The Colonel's voice faltered, "I thank you for your decision to give me your best. Someday Texas will thank you for what you are doing."

The weary Texans returned to their posts and took advantage of the stillness to get some sleep. While they slept Santa Anna's troops were moving into position.

Suddenly, the early dawn erupted with the sound of *"Viva* Santa Anna! *Viva* Santa Anna!"

Drums rolled, and bugles blared.

"They're coming!"

"Santa Anna's coming!"

Texans sprang to their stations. The earth trembled with the impact of thousands of marching feet. Cannons boomed. The noise was deafening!

From his post on the north, Colonel William Travis shouted, "The Mexicans are on us! Give 'em hell, boys!" Travis raised his gun but, before he could fire, a bullet smashed into his forehead. He slumped to the ground, dead.

John Gaston and the others on the wall had no time to reload their guns. The enemy was all around them. The Mexican soldiers climbed up their ladders as soon as they touched the wall. Gaston mustered all the strength he could to push them back. As one toppled to the ground, a bullet hit Gaston in the chest. With one last gasp, he muttered his final words, "I did my best, Ben."

Shell after shell zoomed through the air to slam

into the walls. Gradually, the rock walls around the Alamo began to crumble, leaving a gaping hole in one place. Wave upon wave of Mexican soldiers seized their chance to surge through the opening. The Texans saw them coming and rushed to meet them. When the two forces came face to face, man after man slumped to the ground: Kellogg, Millsaps, Cottle, Floyd, and others.

Galba found his way to Mrs. Dickinson to give her a message but he could not speak. His jaw had been shattered by a bullet. After several attempts to make himself understood, he turned and staggered out to meet his death.

Still Santa Anna's soldiers kept coming. Gradually the Texans' guns were silenced. With their ammunition exhausted, the remaining Texans used their gun butts and knives to fight the Mexican's bayonets. Battling with fierce determination, Dickinson, Bonham, and King were among the last to fall.

And now, a deadly silence covered the courtyard. The first rays of the morning sun filtered down through the haze of smoke and dust that hovered over the battle scene. The dead lay in peace after their heroic efforts.

The battle was over.

In ninety minutes, almost 190 Texans, and over 1500 Mexican soldiers, had met their death.

But the gallant heroes of the Alamo had not died in vain. Their sacrifice had paved the way for Texas liberty. They had gained time for Sam Houston to raise a Texas army.

The thirty-two men from Gonzales and their comrades were now immortal.

BIBLIOGRAPHY

JUVENILE

Laycock, George and Ellen. *How the Settlers Lived,* McKay Company, New York, 1980

Moss, Helen. *Life in a Log Cabin,* Eakin Publications, Burnet, Texas, 1982

ADULT

Alamo DAR Chapter. *The Alamo Heroes and Their Revolutionary Ancestors,* San Antonio, 1976

Bradfield, Jane. *RX, Take One Cannon,* Patrick J. Wagner, Research and Publishing Company, Shiner, Texas, 1981

Cox, Mamie Wynne, *The Romantic Flags of Texas,* Banks Upshaw and Company, Dallas, 1936

DeWitt, Edna. *Lest We Forget,* The Gonzales Inquirer, Gonzales

King, Richard. *Messenger of the Alamo,* Shoal Creek, Austin, 1976

Lord, Walter. *A Time to Stand,* University of Nebraska, Lincoln, Nebraska, 1961

Lukes, Edward. *DeWitt Colony of Texas,* Jenkins Publishing Company, Austin, 1976

Nevin, David. *The Texans,* Time Life Books Publishers, New York, 1975

Smithwick, Noah. *The Evolution of a State,* University of Texas, Austin, 1893

Sheffy, Lester. *Texas,* Banks Upshaw and Company, Dallas, 1954

Tinkle, Lon. *The Alamo,* Signet Books, New York, 1958

MAGAZINE AND PERIODICAL ARTICLES

Bennett, Miles S. "The Battle of Gonzales, The 'Lexington' of The Texas Revolution," *The Quarterly of the Texas State Historical Association,* Volume II, July 1898 to April 1899.

Rosenthal, Phil. "To the Rescue of the Alamo — The Gonzales 32," *True Western Manual.*

Rather, Ethel Zivley. "DeWitt Colony," *The Quarterly of the Texas State Historical Association,* Vol. VIII, October 1904, Number 2

Battle of the Alamo

— DëGolyer Library